THE TWICE EXCEPTIONAL

M.LENNON PERRICONE

© 2014 M. Lennon Perricone.
ISBN-13: 978-0692349304
12-42023v1

Magnetar
info@magnetarpublishing.com

Cover Design
Eno Cirrep Studios

THE TWICE EXCEPTIONAL
M. Lennon Perricone

Acknowledgements
The Cariellos
The Nardones
The Marconis
The Bryrneses
The Warner/Carroccios
Karen Root
And of course, Patti

Twice exceptional: often abbreviated as 2e, refers to intellectually gifted individuals who also have learning disabilities

"The public is wonderfully tolerant. It forgives everything except genius."
—Oscar Wilde—

ONE

It was too cold that winter morning some weeks ago to sit across the street in Central Park and read. Not that I would have anyway. Some stupid tourist or some creepy paparazzi always recognized me. That's the price a woman pays with two best actress Oscars under her belt and a recent third nod.

I was between movies and glad to be back in New York, there's a privacy to New York that LA didn't have. I don't know if people realize how private the twenty fourth floor of the Traymore at Seventy Second Street and Central Park West was. And after such an acrimonious divorce. I needed that privacy. I left my P.A. back in LA to handle things. Between her and my agent Nathan, I was confident everything would be fine.

Enjoying the quiet solicitude of this New York winter, I had decided to catch up on my reading. Reading relaxed me.

My friend, Jenine Gulpilil the most noted American born Australian Aboriginal poet just told her publisher to fuck off. She'd decided to publish her work on her own on some site called U-publish-it. She elaborated that several well-known authors were going that route.

"Publishing your own work is different now," she said. "It has democratized."

She was right, with companies such as U-Publish-it or Write it-Sell it. An author with an established audience could publish their own work and receive five times the royalties from a big publishing house and there was no annoying ten percent to an agent. There were other pluses too, like not having to worry about returns or keeping an inventory.

And that is what put me where I am. Jenine had in a recent work she sent me, had an acknowledgement that read, "To Cyril In-cromona, the most gifted playwright I've ever known."

Who the fuck was Cyril Incromona. I'm a noted actress. I know every living playwright in the world. Curiosity got to me and I looked him up on Amazon. Turns out Mister Incromona was publishing is work himself too and quite a bit of it. There were fourteen plays, six books of poetry and eight novels. I called Jenine and asked her about this Cyril person.

"He's a Phenom," she said. "He has this play, a one-woman show called Standing Beside my Fire. If ever you were meant to play a role Nicole this is the one – order yourself a copy—."

In addition to Standing Beside my Fire, I ordered two of his novels and two more of his plays. The novels, both literary were brilliant, somewhat along the lines of Horatio Alger but not hokey and with far more depth and poignancy. There was a freshness to his language...it was...unencumbered. I'd never read anything like that. Though one of the plays had an uncomfortable level of violence, it was still excellent. A coming-of-age story about a misunderstood artist living on the streets of some fictitious New Jersey city who has his work stolen by a corrupt art dealer, who tries to put another artist's name on that work. Then this young artist strikes back furiously.

'Standing Beside my Fire' was a one woman show about that polarizing writer who had disdain for anything altruistic. I despised her and her oversized novel that from my perspective was nothing more than her own literary dildo. Even after her death, this woman still sold two hundred thousand copies of that book of hers annually.

The play itself was marvelous and the research that had gone into it must have taken forever. As much as I'd hate giving credence to her view of the world. I did very much want to turn this into a biography for the screen. I could play her and I wanted to.

Jenine was expected here for dinner this evening. Nothing fancy, we're just going to order a pizza and chat like girlfriends as we did in college. I was proud of my Jenine, in addition to her Ph.D. and her tenured professor ship at New Brunswick State University, she was the leading voice of American born Australian Aboriginal poetry and she was one of the few poets in the world enjoying commercial and artistic success.

Jenine had taken the Amtrak and arrived earlier than expected. I was glad. I'd been feeling a bit isolated. Her wit and company were something I always looked forward to.

"He's not what you'd think," Jenine said, just after pouring herself another glass of some Long Island red wine.

"Is he one of your students?" I asked her.

"No, in fact he's seems to have disdain for higher education. He says it's an intellectually violent and oppressive oligarchy, I don't know what he means by that."

"You're telling me someone with this level of skill has no formal education?"

"Not only that," she said. "He's only got seven years of schooling. Also, as much as I don't agree with him on almost anything--he's brilliant."

"So, you're saying he's an autodidact."

"He tells me he's a twice exceptional and he'd only found that out recently." "A What?" I said.

"A twice exceptional, I really haven't had the time to research it. I think it means he's gifted."

"So, is he a genius?"

"I don't know," she said. "Though I enjoy his conversations, his friendship and his insights to things, he's a bit guarded about his private life."

"How did you come about meeting someone like that?

As you know, I told New Brunswick State University Press and my agent to kiss my ass. Since I'm now publishing my own stuff, I needed a typesetter. One of my colleagues, a professor Marjorie Carlisle said she knew this guy who was publishing his own stuff and his books looked professional. And she had been paying him to typeset hers. I emailed him and not only does he typeset my books better than any publisher ever did, the covers he designed for me are right from my head. Where's my bag?"

"It's in the guest bedroom." I said, while enjoying a few more sips of wine. She came out with a small book of poems called Chaos from Confusion.

"Look at these filigrees and borders he used," she said. "You think those pricks in the front office of New Brunswick University Press ever gave a shit about the esthetics of my work. No, they were too busy pressuring me to make sure I had it done in time for Black History Month, no matter how many times I told them I'm not African American but an Australian Aboriginal American. Cyril has made reading my poetry a visual experience. Check out the cover its simplicity is perfect."

"She was right; the cover had a yellow background with a back view of a small female child sitting on a hill, staring at a silhouette of a city."

"Do you know how many graphic artists," she said, "have fucked up cover after cover trying to put their signature on my work? Not this guy, he read my poems and comprehended them, asked me a bunch of questions then listened as I read several of them aloud. Not only did I get the cover I wanted, but the one the book needed."

"He sounds like something of an enigma," I said.

"Not only is he an enigma, He's fiercely dogmatic in his views. At the same time, he's got these philosophies about everyday life that are insightful."

"Is he married; does he have a family?"

"No," she said. "He lives alone near the campus. He says people get on his nerves, yet he's charming and personable."

"How old is he?"

"Mid-twenties."

"I'd like to meet him and maybe discuss bringing his work to the screen."

"Let me warn you," she said. "He knows I know you and he's no fan of you, your politics or Hollywood. And he doesn't like movies either."

"He doesn't like movies? I said. "Who the hell doesn't like movies? It's like not liking music."

"He says they're made for and by idiots and they're filmed in a modular format for easy editing."

"That's condescending," I said. "I've dealt with people like that before. They're full of it. They become completely starry eyed around celebrities. Trust me; I will have that arrogant son-of-a-bitch eating out of my hand."

"Darling," Jenine said. "I don't know about that. This guy really marches to his own tone."

"We'll just see about that. I'll have him all Hollywood with the snap of my fingers."

Even on a late Saturday afternoon the forty-mile drive from Manhattan to New Brunswick, was unpleasant. Not wanting to be conspicuous,

I decided against a limousine and rented a car instead. After jockeying for position in the Lincoln tunnel, I had to contend with the cursed New Jersey Turnpike. Then a detour forced me to drive through the local New Brunswick Streets.

I couldn't believe how much the small city that I'd spent so much of my college years in had changed. There were high rises all over George Street. And the skyline was much more expansive.

Jenine lived in a large restored Victorian on Livingston Avenue. One of the pluses of visiting Jenine, I got to drive passed New Brunswick's theater district, the most important theater district in the New York area outside of Manhattan, such plays as David Auburn's Pulitzer Prize Winning Proof got their start there and there was the famed tony award winning African American theater company Crossroads.

I couldn't pull into Jenine's driveway there was another car in it. She had cautioned me that she'd have her usual Saturday crowd there. In case they hadn't dispersed, she'd leave the front door open so I could enter and discreetly wait in the dining room for them to clear out.

After parking the rental across the street, I entered Jenine's eclectic home. Books were piled everywhere and her dining room table was filled with artifacts from trips to Kenya, New

Guinea and her most recent excursion to Australia's outback to get in touch with her aboriginal roots.

Standing in the shadows of the dining room through an archway, I could see into about a quarter of the living room and I could hear raising voices of a heated discussion.

"Nobody has the right to obligate me to anything or anyone." A male voice said.

"Nonsense!" an agitated female voice answered. "We are all in this together!"

"The hell we are," the male voice shouted. "You and your ilk have used that false concept to pilferage everything. You have no right to obligate me to anyone. My life belongs to me."

"My Ilk, my Ilk," the female voice was growing louder. "It's your Ilk that would leave someone bleeding in the gutter!"

"Here we go again," the male voice shouted. "No, I would not nor would my...as you said it...ilk. You're Ilk, rather than helping someone bleeding in the gutter would instead blame my ilk for it and demand my ilk take care of it. Nobody has any right to determine where my benevolence goes. That's up to me."

"Wrong buddy," she said. "That breeds elitism. There has to be some sort of equity."

"Hey!" The male voice interjected. My ilk isn't the elite. Yours is and it's the most condescending and elitist ilk that ever existed."

"How can someone concerned with altruism be an elitist?"

"Because you demand others make sacrifices, by force if necessary. That is elitism."

"Crap!" she shouted. "The greedy rich need to contribute their fair share."

"And the lazy poor," he answered. "Need to start pulling their own weight!"

"How dare you make such a blanket statement?" There was now a sneering tone to the female voice.

Why not!" he said. "You just made one. You assume anyone who has wealth is greedy. So, if you can assume productive beings are avaricious. I can assume the so-called down at heal are lazy."

"How could you speak like that about the poor?"

"I got news for you Professor, the poor, as you call them are not sacrosanct, nor are they innocuous."

"Sorry Guys," I heard Jenine's voice interject. "I hate to interrupt your weekly verbal bloodbath, but Cyril here has a meeting so we need to wrap this up."

I moved a bit closer to the living room and I noticed Jenine and an elderly woman standing next to a young man whose face I could see clearly. It was a good face, handsome…striking. One could tell he was part Italian. His eyes were dark and his skin was fair but not pink. There was a tightness to his mouth but it didn't make him look severe, but rather intense and it accented his square jaw. His hair was dark, thick and wavy and his face was framed by the red turtleneck sweater he wore.

"Thank you so much Cyril," the elderly woman said as she affectionately put her hand on his arm. "You did such a beautiful job on my novel and the cover is perfect. You have to let me take you to lunch."

"That isn't necessary Professor, you've already paid me."

"Oh please, I insist," she said. "How about Friday."

"Ok," he said. "But you have to pick the place."

"I can't wait!" she said. "I'll see you during the week Jenine. Good luck with your potential new client Cyril."

I watched as she turned to Jenine and said. "It's invigorating to have my work belong to me again and not have to be subject to one of the those editing butchers at my former publisher and it's so nice to be able to use and occasional adverb and semicolon again. And the royalties are so much better too. Stay warm Cyril its cold out there." The elderly professor affectionately pecked him on his cheek.

"I promise."

"If I was younger and single Cyril... what I wouldn't do to you." The elderly woman was putting her coat on when she turned to Cyril and said. "Before I forget darling, Professor Neworth is going to call you, he's just finished his manuscript and wants to put it on U-Publish-it."

"Great," Cyril replied. "Another book smart liberal parrot."

"I doubt it, "she said. "Professor Neworth is attached to the School of Engineering and his manuscript is about fly fishing in New York State."

So that's him, I thought. Not what I expected. When one hears someone is gifted, one expects an eccentric look, and has difficulty when someone of that nature looks.... normal, even well put together.

"I thought she'd never leave," I heard Jenine say to him.

"Hey, I love professor Carlisle. So, when is this mysterious client you want me to meet getting here?"

"She's Already here. Before you meet her Cyril, I need to qualify something. She's not here because she needs you to typeset her manuscript. She's an actress friend of mine and she's expressed an interest in Standing Beside my Fire"

"To what end?" I heard him answer cautiously.

"That's between you and her."

I feel shanghaied. Let's get this crap over with. Where is she?"

I would be lying if I said I didn't use my celebrity to sway people. A coquettish smile and an acknowledgment of their name would have most people eating out of my hand.

He walked into the dining room and I could tell by the expression on his face he recognized me. It was an acknowledgement nothing else, this young man was not impressed with who I was.

"Hi Ms. Davenport, I'm Cyril," he said politely.

"Nicole," I said. "Call me Nicole."

"I thought you were here because you needed me to design a cover or typeset your manuscript. Jenine informs me you have some other intentions."

"Why don't I make you two some coffee," Jenine said, and I knew this was strategic to distract Cyril. "Then I'll head over to the market and leave you two to sort things out."

"Sure," he said. "When have I ever refused your coffee Jenine?"

With Jenine out of the way, we sat in her living room and it was unnerving to me that this young man had made no attempt to acknowledge me professionally or commented on my work.

"If I can be candid," I said to him.

"By all means," He replied.

"Jenine tells me you're a...a... twice exceptional. I have to say you're not what I was expecting."

Before he responded, he chuckled a bit. "What were you expecting, John Forbes from a Beautiful Mind or Raymond Babbit from Rain Man? I'm not some delusional genius or some idiot savant. I'm as you just said a twice exceptional. That means I can write a seventy-thousand-word novel in about two months and I can write a thirteen-thousand-word stage play in two weeks. In simple terms, I've been evaluated as a highly gifted individual who is burdened with Dyscalculia, which means I have near complete paralysis when it comes to mathematics."

"That's interesting," I said.

"I'm not finished, I also have dysgraphia, though all of my punctuation is correct. Thirty percent of the words I write will be misspelled and several key words, along with articles and conjunctions will be left out. I will never see that because I wrote it. If someone else however wrote like that, I'd notice it immediately. In addition, I am pretty much crippled when it comes to writing in long hand. That has cause people to label me as lazy and uncaring about my learning most of my life."

"Wait a minute!" I said. "I read some of your plays and novels they were perfect. You must have one hell of an editor."

"I'm my own editor."

"You just said."

"Like many challenged or handicapped people, I have prosthetics, the first one is a calculator and the second one is a computer. Things like grammar check, spell check and text to speech allow me to correct my work. I've always learned by listening, if I can hear it. I can correct it. When I play back my work on text to speech. I can proof read it and fix it."

"Is it difficult for you to read Cyril?"

No, I read quite a bit. I have dysgraphia and I have dyscalculia. I'm not dyslexic."

"How the hell do you typeset for all these professors?"

"QuarkXPress is technology, I'm not writing. I'm just setting words and paragraphs in book form."

"The cover designs?" I asked.

"I've always had an esthetic eye."

I could tell he was growing impatient.

"I'm sure an important celebrity like you," he said. "Didn't come here incognito from Manhattan to discuss my shortcomings."

"I didn't, I came here to discuss Standing Beside My Fire. If I can be candid, I have an interest in it."

"Why?"

His question threw me off.

"It's difficult, I said "for a woman to find a role of substance."

"You do know who it's about," he said.

"Of course."

"Your political activism is diametrically opposed to anything she stood for. Why would you want to give her views a public platform?"

"Didn't Jane Fonda play Nancy Reagan? Though I may disagree with the protagonist of your play, she was still a woman who has legions of devotees. They'd flock to see a movie about her..."

"Movie," there was apprehension in his voice. "This is written for the stage. I don't write screenplays."

"You won't have to; all you have to do is sell me the film rights and with the right script doctor..."

"There are no film rights," he said.

"I'm sorry, maybe you don't understand." I answered. "You let me option the rights to make a film, then I will get financing."

"I understand you perfectly; there are no film rights because I will never allow any of my plays to be made into movies."

"Look you don't have to negotiate right now. I promise I won't low ball you and all I want at this moment is the option..."

"Did you hear what I just said, this is a play, and there isn't enough money in the world. I don't like current movies. Their choppy and they lack literature and in within a year all of them end up in the five-dollar DVD bin at Walmart. No, I've seen what Hollywood can do to a play once they get their greedy hands on it. Look at the damage done to Proof and Spinning into Butter. Never mind the complete destruction of Agnes of God, and the hatchet job done to William Inge's Bus Stop so it could become a vehicle for Marilyn Monroe. Sorry...Nicole ...If you want to produce Standing by My Fire for the stage, we can a have a conversation. In the meantime, I should get to work.... I can tell by your face; you are wondering what a twice exceptional does for a living. Aside from my typesetting. I'm an usher at the Livingston Avenue Theatre and a freelance telemarketer."

"You're leaving?" I shouted. "This could bring you out of your poverty."

"Poverty? I don't live in poverty I'm doing just fine," he said.

"Aren't you a starving playwright?"

"So, your intention is to exploit me."

"What! No...."

"Listen," he said. "I may not be able to understand long division and complex multiplications but I know how and where to invest the nest egg my great aunt left me. And I'm far from starving. Now if you'll excuse me The Livingston Avenue Theatre needs me the late afternoon matinee of Moon for the Misbegotten."

"Can't somebody cover for you?" I shouted. "I came here from Manhattan."

"With all due respect Nicole, you came here under false pretenses. I thought you needed typesetting. I'm sorry but if I don't leave now. I'll be late."

This sucks, I thought. This little shit left me standing in Janine's living room like a jilted bride.

TWO

In the two weeks that passed since my encounter with Cyril Incromona. I was unable to get him out of my mind. I ordered his full canon of plays and novels. I didn't get to the novels but the plays were brilliant and unique. Several were about misunderstood gifted people. Others were difficult relationships between family members. Some were written to get his political and economic philosophies across. All expressed his unique voice. One that stuck out with poignancy was King's' Knight 4. It was all about an underachieving youth in a reform school who becomes that school's chess champion, then takes on and defeats a chess champion from a prestigious private boarding school.

Adding to this play's intensity, no chess was played it was only implied and inferred. In the end when the protagonist wins, I wanted to stand up and cheer.

Another thing impressing me, unlike some well-established playwrights, Cyril really knew staging. I wondered how he knew that. Then I remembered, he ushered at one of the nation's leading theaters. He said he learned by listening. I deduced that's how and where he learned staging. This enigma Cyril Incromona was resourceful.

As touching and as enjoyable as his other works were. I kept going back to Standing Beside My Fire. I hated that woman and what she stood for but Cyril's play focused on her struggle as an immigrant, her work and her unwillingness to compromise. As much as I hated to admit it. She never did. And though I found them offensive. She was a woman of principles.

Years of playing stoic mothers, rigid business women and soft-hearted hookers, had left me jaded. I needed this role. It would take me out of my comfort zone and challenge me as an artist, if I still was an artist.

I'd been communicating with my agent back and forth about Cyril and he pretty much told me to forget about it. People not from the business didn't understand our hierarchy and were always trouble. A prime example of that he said. "If this little shit doesn't want any money there's something not right with him."

Thinking he was right, I tried over the next few days to put Cyril and his play out of my mind. I couldn't.

I noticed the time—midmorning. That's when nostalgia over took me, and I decided to make another trip to New Jersey but not in a car. I'd put on a winter hat, wear no makeup and with my darkest glasses, I'd take the train, as I did when I was a student at New Brunswick State. For some reason I needed to slip into Cyril's world. Maybe that would help me understand his resistance to allowing me to option his play.

It was a mistake taking the train. Unlike in my younger days before cell phones, when a train ride was quiet and almost reflective. Now, everybody was talking or texting and it irritated me that so many phones kept ringing. Armed with Cyril's address that I got from Jenine and with the winter dampness chilling me to my bones. I started walking the half mile from the Train Station to his address on George Street. Though the small city around it had changed dramatically since my days at New Brunswick State, George Street with its upscale restaurants next to dive bars and discount stores still felt the same and one knew one was in a college town.

I crossed New Street. This was where the newer and more upscale high-rise apartments

29

were. Cyril's address was one of these buildings. Again, not what I expected. I assumed him to live in a room in one of the old frame houses. Another surprise pertaining to young Mister Incromona. Then I remembered him saying he'd inherited a nest egg.

A hundred-dollar bill and a smile from a celebrity will get you passed any doorman. I'd asked him if Cyril was home, he said yes, he'd come down for his mail about fifteen minutes ago.

Just before I found myself ringing the bell at apartment 11e. I debated whether to forget the whole thing, turn around, close up my New York digs, head back to LA and do one of the four romantic comedies being pitched to my agent. Too late, I rang the bell.

"Nicole," a surprised Cyril said. "What are you doing here?"

"Do you have some time, we kind of parted abruptly at our last encounter and I thought maybe we could chat."

"Sure," he said. "Come on in. "Would you like some coffee?"

"That would be nice," I said.

I gazed around the apartment It was immaculate with a distant odor of cleaners. Everything was in order. I'd been doing some reading on twice exceptionals and one of the things many of them suffer with is disorganization, not this one.

Everything in the apartment, its furnishings, and its wall decorations were done in varying shades of silver and gray, including a silver laptop on a gray desk in front of a living room window, that looked out over the changing skyline of New Brunswick.

I observed the screen, I could tell by the format, Cyril was working on a novel. Nearly every third word had a red line under it and every sixth or seventh word had a blue line underneath it too. This is how he must work, I thought. He writes it then goes back and fixes it.

"I could dictate to the computer," he said from the kitchen. "But I find that exhausting."

"It looks interesting," I said.

"It's a pro-capitalist science fiction novel. I spent a year learning physics before I started writing it."

"This is a lovely apartment," I said, feeling guilty at being discovered.

"Thanks, I rented it with my former fiancé. She was going to graduate school here at New Brunswick, her father, who hated me decided she should study back in Seoul and without me."

"I'm sorry, I said. "Was it a messy break up?"

"Totally."

Next to the television, I saw a trophy with a chess pawn on top of it.

"You're a chess champion…."

"I was during my reform school days," he said. "I don't play much anymore."

I continued looking at the room. There were wall shelves; on them were DVDs of every Shakespeare play, a rare production of Medea, and a large collection of audiobooks ranging from Karl Marx to Aristotle.

Then there were his books. Jack London, Ayn Rand, Earnest Hemingway, Henry Miller and Jack Williamson. It wasn't limited to them on another shelf was Ralph Ellison, Richard Right and Zora Neale Hurston. Then there were poets: Whitman, Byron, Plath, Shelly and several plays and poetry volumes by Miguel Pinero.

On the next shelf were the Blu-rays of every recorded version of Wagner's Ring. Next to them were the CD versions of those same ring cycles.

There was something artistically and intellectually powerful about this perplexing young man.

"Reform school?" I said. Bringing myself back to reality.

"We all have a past, he said."

"And we all have a future," I added.

"I assume," he said, as he entered the living room with two mugs of coffee. "That's some sort of a proposition relating to Standing by My Fire?"

"You must have great admiration and affection for her to compose something so detailed. Don't you want to pay homage to her?"

"Not in a film, it's a stage work."

"I'm having trouble comprehending this," I said. "You're an unknown playwright and an unknown writer. Why wouldn't you want to bring recognition to your work?"

"My work is on Amazon, if anyone wants it, they can find it there."

"How the hell are they going to find it if they don't know who you are?" "You did."

"Touché," I said.

"Nicole," he said. "I'm flattered you love my work. But understand I don't like the way current movies are made. Currently scripts are written to support action or the actors. It's not a writer friendly medium. And they're hasn't' been a well written dramatic script since Crash."

"I see you have a copy, And some other well written movies, All about Eve, Splendor in the grass."

Mostly, when their done well," he said. "I like plays set to film."

"Well now," I tried.

"Don't even go there," he said. "There is no possible way to turn a one-woman character play set in a living room into a movie."

"We'd add Characters..."

"No, you won't, that's why I can't let you do the movie."

"Cyril," I said, "it can make you rich."

"I'm not looking for money."

Not wanting to push it. I let the conversation change. During that change, I ask Cyril why he did plays and not screenplays.

He replied. "Before my mom got real sick. My great aunt purchased for her a DVD of an old movie from the 1930's they'd use to watch together on VHS. My mother never got around to opening it. Out of curiosity, I put it on. It was this wonderful yarn about these two women, they ran a school for girls, and this evil little girl who accuses one of them of what at the time was considered immorality. I was glued to it.

Then came this powerful confrontation in that little girl's grandmother's living room with those two women. I kept rewinding it. Every word had a specific function to move the story forward. I would later learn that was the Tilford living room scene in act two scene one of Lillian Hellman's 'The Children's Hour.' I also found out many other writers didn't respect Miss Hellman's ability. I did, and I was hooked. From then on, all I watched were plays set to film or films closely based on plays."

"Lillian Hellman was an unapologetic and committed Stalinist," I said. "She'd be a sworn enemy to the protagonist of your play..." Cyril cut me off.

"Why do people of your political persuasion always do that?"

"Do what!" I answered.

"If someone doesn't follow your orthodoxy, you find there's something lacking in their character. You're assuming I shouldn't like Lillian Hellman as a playwright because she was a communist. Since I do, you think I'm not secure in my beliefs."

"I beg your pardon," I said. "I'm here trying to convince you to let me play a woman who—I on any political level despise."

His phone chirped and he answered a text. "Speaking of plays," he said. "A group of students from the university are doing a reading of one of mine. I'd be flattered if you'd join me."

"I'd loved to, do you think my presence..."

"Theater is always dark and you can stand in the kitchen. It's off to the side and nobody can see you and it's only a reading so all I need to do is hear it."

It was flurrying as we walked down George Street heading for some church basement located on Neilson and Bayard. I hadn't been on Bayard Street in decades. I couldn't help myself as I walked with Cyril, I put my arm in his and he didn't mind at all.

"You know these are my old stomping grounds when I was at Lawrence Gilmore School of the arts," I said.

"Why did you abandon theater?" he asked me.

"I didn't," I said. "It was only one part of my career. I could accuse you of the same thing, what are you writing in that apartment back there?"

"My sci fi novel."

"If you as a playwright can grant yourself the privilege of writing novels. I, as an actor have the same right to do movies."

"It's not the same thing," he said.

"Yes, it is," I answered. "You just don't like current movies. Look kid what I'm about to say is far more in line with the way you think than I do. It's ok for an artist to make money."

"Not if they compromise the integrity of their work."

"Getting paid for doing what you do to fill an empty belly," I answered. "Is not a compromise of one's integrity? Some of the most creative people I've known kid were commercial artists, script doctors, and scene and set designers and they were all well paid for what they did. Does that make them any less creative...no. Even in the first major novel written by the subject of your play, doesn't the protagonist get paid for his work?"

"But he never compromises it. He stands against multitudes who hate him for not compromising. He doesn't let them beat him. He even stops doing what he loves rather than compromise."

I stopped in my tracks and withdrew my arm from his. "Are you impugning my integrity?" I sneered.

"Of course not, I'm just saying an artist has to always maintain standards. Though I don't like current movies and in all candor that includes most of the movies you've made this decade, that has nothing to do with your performances. I know what you've turned down. And I know you are a great actress. And as many movies as you made.

You are still one of the few in current filmography that is an actor before a movie star. If you weren't you wouldn't be pestering me about my play. I got invited to a writer's conference once. There must have been hundreds of writers there and there were literary agents, publishers and published novelist. All these would be writers were all bragging they had the next this or they had the next that. They're all lining up to pitch their work and I, of course pitched mine. And as you've gathered, I'm no shrinking violet. They weren't interested in my work and I was glad, because I didn't want these people anywhere near what I...that's right what—I created. It's mine. If someone wants to read my stuff great, if someone wants to stage it according to my guidelines great. If someone hates it great, if someone wants to rip it to pieces great, but it will always be mine. We need to get moving again. Deb the director gets all pissed off when I'm not there on time."

He made his point and took my arm and we rushed into the basement of that church. An annoyed middle-aged woman approached, then noticed me and her face lit up. Before she could say anything, Cyril spoke up.

"Sorry I'm late Deb, my cousin Phoebe here from Virginia isn't familiar with New Brunswick, she got lost and I had to guide her here."

"Phoebe?" The woman said disappointed. "Did anyone ever tell you; you look like Nicole ..."

"I get that all the time; I said in a mock southern accent. "If only I had her money."

"If only we all did. They're ready Cyril." Deb said.

Cyril's play, was gut wrenching. It was the fictionalized accounting of the actual lynching of

Italian immigrant grocers in a southern state for allowing African Americans to shop in their stores. The play centered on one of the families who'd had shopped in the store and were now hiding one of the grocer's terrified teenaged sons.

The father of this African American family, fearing trouble wanted to send him away. The mother refused to yield. Eventually an angry trio shows up. Convinced they're not hiding the missing youth.

The trio decides to torment this African American family. They beat the father senseless, and when they're about to gang rape the mother, the Italian youth to defend her, sneaks out of hiding with an axe and kills the trio.

The family and youth bury the trio and the young Italian escapes and the African American family are able to go on unencumbered. Its level of violence aside, this was a well-crafted play that said something without pontificating. It also showed the clarity of Cyril's voice.

I never knew about this incident involving the lynching of Italian immigrants and that meant a visit to Wikipedia. The small audience made up of students, professor Carlisle, some church members and the African American pastor where roused to their feet. Cyril took a modest bow and I realized he was right. I had gotten away from the artistry of my craft. I was more concerned with ticket sales, my next project, and promoting myself. It was imperative that I bring Standing by My Fire to the screen now more than ever to salvage my integrity as an actor.

I observed in the near distance Professor Carlisle chatting with Cyril. I couldn't make out what they were saying, but they were both grinning. She said her good byes and as the audience dispersed, Cyril approached me.

I hugged him in congratulations and said. "You have such a gift for dialogue."

"That's because at heart," he said. "I'm a pompous ass who won't shut up."

I reminded myself how important dialogue was to a story and Cyril had been right that dialogue with expression of the writer's individuality had been all but removed from current American films. He was also correct when he said this play had to be listen to.

"Cyril," I said. "I haven't' been so moved by anything in a long time."

"Thank you," he replied uncomfortable about the compliment.

THREE

I woke next to Cyril feeling feminine and girlish. Tender, Impetuous and loaded with stamina, Cyril was delicious to make love with. After his play reading, the snow was really coming down and before we got back to his apartment, we ordered takeout Chinese, I couldn't remember the last time I waited in a Chinese restaurant for spare ribs, chicken with broccoli and egg drop soup.

In his apartment, watching the nighttime snow fall on New Brunswick, I learned much about Cyril: Born in the Bensonhurst section of Brooklyn. As I suspected, he was only half Italian American. His mother was Russian American and was a paranoid schizophrenic. She was institutionalized then died in that institution.

His father, a Mafia wanna-be who he had nothing to do with was serving a life sentence for a botched contract killing.

Cyril was raised on an off by his mother's aunt. She herself was sickly and had difficulty relating to and controlling an adolescent male.

I asked him how he ended up in reform school. He told me he was a chronic truant. He had gotten fed up with as he put it. "Always ending up in classes filled with thugs and idiots." After reform school, he said, he never set foot in a classroom again. To survive, he told me he mostly worked as a telemarketer. Then when he was twenty-one. His aunt passed leaving him his nest egg and he decided to pursue his playwriting.

Still sleeping, Cyril stirred and I looked over at him noticing the picture of Jessica Kim, his former fiancé.

After their breakup, Cyril told me, because of the small theater district here. He decided to stay in New Brunswick, and then the professors came a calling for typesetting and his book covers.

I got up and went into his living room and looked at his shelf again—this time in more detail. There was a little book of poems about sixty pages that was written by him called Peace from Delusion. Some were written in his early youth.

Most were painful commentaries about a misunderstood young man who, to me was sometimes lonely but had learned to be alone.

"I haven't written any poetry in a long time." Cyril said, standing in a gray robe at the corridor that led to the bedroom from the living room.

"Aren't you cold" he said, "and it's still a bit dark and there's no treatment on that window. With the light on somebody from one of the other buildings might see you naked. We don't want something like that going viral on the internet."

"It wouldn't matter," I told him. "I've already been in the buff in several movies."

Suddenly I felt naked; not in an embarrassing way but in that free sense you have when you have an intimate connection with someone.

"Here," he said as he threw me another one of his robes. "It's still early the heat hasn't come up yet."

"Cyril your poetry, it's so compelling."

"It's ok, poetry for me is a cop out. I write it when I'm stuck and I don't really enjoy writing it. I'm a fiction writer."

"Would you mind if I kept this little volume?" "I'd be honored," he said.

"Would you sign it?"

"Of course, how kind of you to ask."

"You're such a renaissance man," I said. "Novels, plays, poems, and chess."

"Chess, I do more poetry than I do chess,"

Cyril didn't know I'd read his chess play and I wanted to hear for myself how much of it was true and to what level it might be embellished.

"Cyril," I said. "How does a boy become a chess champion in a reform school?"

"It's the same story that has dogged me my whole life. When I arrived at that reform school, they gave me a bunch of tests. And of course, as it always happens. I could tell they were confounded by my high reading level my vocabulary, and knowledge of what word meant what, and my complete inability to spell, write or do any real math.

I could see it in their faces they didn't know what to make of me academically. Once I got into the general population, I heard one of the cottages housed the smart guys. It was called brainiac central. Of course, they didn't place me in that cottage. As was the case with all the schools I attended. I was placed with kids whom intellectually, I'd have nothing in common.

To their credit, my cottage brothers saw something in me before anyone. This guy Jamal from Bed-Sty kept saying to me you're smart, smarter than any of those brainiacs in that cottage and you need to play chess. I wasn't interested. He insisted almost to the point of threatening me with his posse. He wouldn't leave me alone till finally I gave in to get him to stop annoying me. He taught me and I took to it right away. Soon I was playing two or three guys in my cottage at the same time.

All my cottage brothers' start chanting my name and saying. 'We're taking the fucking chess challenge this year. We got the guy; we're taking those mother fuckers down.' In four months was the annual chess challenge and this smug cottage had taken it ever since it started twenty years earlier.

This year, they had this guy Rashad Smith, he was supposedly the best they ever had. I hated his fucking guts. He made fun of my handwriting and said I wrote like a two-year-old and he asked me if I was retarded. Now I had a dog in this fight. I played chess six, sometimes seven times a night. When my cottage brothers weren't available, I played against the computer. I read whatever there was in the library about chess. Whenever I had access to the internet, I surfed it and absorbed everything I could about the game.

The challenge comes around and every guy who knew how to play signed up, maybe sixty seventy, a real diverse mosaic of guys. Four guys from the smart cottage immediately take the lead and they're being really arrogant about it too.

They don't notice I'm right behind them. In fact, nobody but my cottage brothers are paying any attention to me. All of a sudden there's only seven guys left and somebody notices I'm the only one left that's not from that cottage and I'm in third place. Not only that, Rashad and I are the only two that haven't lost a game yet.

Come Monday, my cottage brothers are bragging all over the place. I have four days before the finals on Saturday and its everywhere I'm in contention. Teachers are congratulating me, guys from other cottages are telling me I need to take those condescending motherfuckers down. Saturday rolls around I'm ready, I'm feeling pumped.

I walk into the auditorium and you would have thought it was the Super Bowl. There are feeds of the games on screens so everyone in the crowd could watch. And everybody's there, all the guys from all the cottages, the teachers, the janitors, and even the people from the front office.

There's four of us in contention. Me, two other jerks and Rashad. We're playing best out of three. One game, then two games and it's down to Rashad and me and he's under enormous pressure. His cottage has never lost the chess challenge, and he knows he could be the first one ever to lose it to another cottage. I also knew I better not take him for granted. This guy's got the highest IQ on property and he's the school's academic superstar.

First game's a slugfest but I take it. I checkmate him with my two rooks. The second game he's all nervous, I get his queen by the fifth move. I fucking have him. He's losing, he knows it and he's sweating like a pig. The room is dead quiet. He makes another mistake and I get one of his rooks.

I sneak a glance at his cottage brothers and his prefect. They're in a silent panic. The smartest guy on property is about to fall to a guy who can't do long division and has to endure the embarrassment of Sister Agnes's math workshop.

Next move he makes he tries to trap my queen. I set him up for that, three moves earlier and he took the bait...fucking idiot. Checkmate! I shut the mother fucker out. He never beat me. The whole auditorium, except his cottage stands and cheers. While that's going on I catch a glance at Jamal, he's not cheering just smiling. For the rest of the night all I heard from him was 'I told you, you could do it, and I knew you were smarter than those nerds in that cottage.'

After he was discharged, I realized something. The first person to recognize my intellect and force me to take hold of it was a fifteen-year-old wannabe rapper from Bed-Sty. What I owe that kid."

"What happened to him," I asked.

"I don't know. I never saw or heard from him again. I hope he did good."

The only difference I could see from Cyril's play, and what he recounted was the antagonist chess player was from a fancy boarding school.

Then another thought popped into my head. Cyril was in many ways the perfect storm for a writer. The upheavals and adversity in his life was providing him with an endless amount of material for plays, novels and even poetry.

"You have no idea," he said. "What it's like to feel smart and stupid at the same time."

"Stupid," I said. "Cyril how could you of all people feel stupid?"

"I've often felt stupid. And I've often been called stupid. It's no fun when you have to void out three or four checks in front of someone before you get it right. You can be the most brilliant person in the world. If you can't do math, people think you're a fucking idiot. Illiterates who are good at math are always considered to have high levels of native intelligence. But schmucks like me who can't write in long hand or multiply are considered bottom feeders on the learning curve."

"If you're dopey," I said. "How did you learn so much?"

"I'm my own best teacher. I know how I have to learn and that's how I address it. The easiest way for me to learn something is to explore it and figure it out. And that is a far more intimate way of learning. You'll get an insight to things that nobody with traditional learning ever has, because it's just the academic version of fast food. Here it is, now eat it.

But when you learn on your own, you dig deeper and deeper till you understand things and that's the greatest instructor of all. Let me give you an example. Another factor of my shortcomings, I can't read aloud, not even my own work after it's corrected. It's the one area I hadn't gotten control of, so I volunteered as a lector in my Church. I'd have to study what I was reading for two hours before I could get on the podium. But I did it. I read aloud in my church for two years. I conquered it."

I became angry with all of this and I had to ask him. "Didn't any of your teachers notice this?"

"The first time I ever wrote my name was in first grade," he said. "I wrote if from right to left. The only thing the teacher said was 'Cyril you wrote your name backwards.' It was downhill from there. Please understand in other areas I excelled, so they assumed I was just lazy.

Whenever I took notes in school, if they weren't done on a computer, I couldn't read them back and I'd fail. Miss Hockstein did not allow computers in her science class, nope; notes had to be taken by hand. But she was a good lecturer and since I learn by listening, I managed to pass that class. For a time, I wondered if I was illiterate."

"My God Cyril," I said. "With all that, you still became a prolific writer."

FOUR

fter a week with Cyril. I had to get back to Manhattan. I hated leaving him, but a temp agency called and needed him for a telemarketing assignment and he wanted to get a new television, so he took it. These four days later the two of us spoke at length on the phone, he was still adamant no film rights for Standing Beside my Fire.

What I did next, I did with only the best intentions. I felt Cyril was an undiscovered talent the world needed to know. With my agent Nathan now here in New York, I invited him over and I gave him copies of several of Cyril's plays. I let him know, I wanted very much to create a film of Standing Beside my Fire. He seemed skeptical as he warned me again about people

51

not from the business. But he'd put out some feelers about financing.

I never expected what happened next. Nathan called all flustered. Several production companies were ready to go with Standing Beside My Fire, if I would sign on to the project. They also made it clear a one-person character movie would never work. The part of her husband and several other characters in her life would have to be written in.

Then things got worse. One of my rivals had heard Nathan was shopping the script on my behalf. She got a hold of it on line, and was trying to shop it too, never bothering to get Cyril's approval or permission.

Nathan, sounding exhausted told me other players, both in front of the camera and behind it, had gotten Cyril's work off Amazon and were pitching it to anyone who'd listen. Cyril had become the hottest writer in Hollywood.

I didn't know how to react to what Nathan said next. Skyscraper Studios, the largest studio in the business was offering fifteen million dollars for rights to Cyril's entire canon. The movie industry, like the publishing industry wanted what it couldn't have.

I felt sick; I realized these people didn't want Cyril's work because of its literary merit.

No, they wanted it because I wanted it and that meant its only value came from the ability to get it away from me and into their greedy hands. For just this reason, there are piles of wonderful scripts that have been purchased that never again see the light of day.

"Who is this guy?" Nathan shouted into the phone. "Does he have representation? I'd add him to my client list in a heartbeat."

One saving grace through all of this, Cyril was his own publisher and there was no contact information listed anywhere in anything he published. That made him difficult but not impossible to get in touch with.

"Nathan," I said, "I thought you didn't like people from outside the business."

"I'll make an exception. There's fifteen million dollars on the table. I want to represent him. There' hasn't been a screen writer this hot since Robert Towne."

"He doesn't write screenplays," I said. "He's a playwright."

"Six of one, half dozen of another. Everyone's starts out as an artist, till they get their first big paycheck, then its sell to the highest bidder and we got the highest bidder. I want to take a meeting with him. You know what ten percent of fifteen million is. I want you to arrange it. I'll be in New York again by the end of the week. I'll see you then."

After Nathan hung up, my head was spinning. Every other person on this planet would be thrilled to have someone offer them fifteen million dollars for their work. Cyril would consider it an invasion of his privacy and would be irritated by it. Worse, if I hooked him up with Nathan, he'd know I'd shopped his work around behind his back. And with fifteen million dollars hovering somebody was going to find a way to get to Cyril.

Another problem, all feelings aside, I desperately wanted that role and Cyril was the only thing standing in the way of me getting it. This didn't make me feel good. Cyril was not unhappy the way his life was going. These sharks wouldn't care about him one bit.

Putting all of this out of my mind. I began opening the day's mail. Only my private mail came here, my bills and fan letters were delivered to whomever took care of such things. There wasn't much in the pile, a circular from the local Food Emporium, one from Dagastino's, a form letter from the building's property management company. And a card from Cyril. I could tell it was from him by the childlike writing on the envelope. I was both afraid and excited to open it. Inside was a poem, written in his own hand for me. ...How personal—how intimate—, I thought.

I was unable to read it. The letters that I could make out were capital and. Most if not all of the words were misspelled or so badly written they may as well have been.

Cyril...being Cyril, enclosed in the envelope, a typed version of the poem. I put it in my wallet. I decided I always wanted it with me.

Nathan had arrived in New York a day earlier than expected. I sat down with him at a Perkies coffee bar on Amsterdam.

"Skyscraper is ready to go as high as sixteen million on the entire canon. Everybody's talking, everybody's downloading, and everybody's ordering hard copies. It seems your friend's got a screenplay for everyone."

"There not screenplays," I said. "Their stage plays."

"Screen, stage. It doesn't matter. What matters is you want one and that means everyone wants one and we can get them."

"What about just Standing Beside My Fire?" I asked.

"One million, but only if they get the options on the rest of his properties. By the way, I thought he'd be here."

"No Nathan, he's in New Jersey."

"New Jersey? What the hell's he doing in New Jersey?"

"He lives there."

"Nobody lives in New Jersey."

"He does."

"Is he coming?"

"No Nathan, he's not. I haven't mentioned any of this to him."

"I guess this means we have to get our asses to New Jersey," he said.

"He's not expecting us."

Nathan gave me a stern look. "Darling, you may be at the top of the pile right now. A major studio, in fact the major of the majors wants these properties and they're willing to get you Standing by My Fire, if they get the rest...you better play ball."

The traffic on the turnpike was a nightmare. Several times while we slowed down, the thought of running out of the limo and forgetting everything popped into my head. I had come to a terrible realization about my life. Unlike Cyril, who the work meant everything.

With me, it was no longer about the work and it was no longer about the results from that work. It was instead about my brand and how much collective revenue that brand could generate for others and me.

I found myself in a biting moral dilemma. If I convinced Cyril to take the deal, that would satisfy the studio get me my movie and, in the process, makes Cyril rich. This should be a win-win situation. But Cyril had changed the equation; his work meant everything to him. By proxy, it meant everything to me.

"He must live around here somewhere," Nathan said bringing me back to reality. For some reason his presence was annoying me. I've never realized the mercenary he was before. We were now at Cyril's building and the concierge, familiar with me, allowed us to go right up.

"Cyril, it's me,"

I could hear him unlocking the door and my heart was beating rapidly.

"Hey," he said. As he opened the door. "What the heck are you doing here?"

I could see the concern in his face as he noticed that I was with Nathan. Realizing his apprehension, I said.

"Cyril this is Nathan, he's, my agent."

A smile came across Cyril's face. And he said, "Hey, it's a pleasure to meet you."

"The pleasure my young friend, is all mine," Nathan said.

I could tell by Nathan's demeanor; he was up to something.

"I don't have any coffee, but I have some wine only white. Would you like a glass?" Cyril said.

"That would be lovely Cyril," I said.

"I'm sorry," Nathan said. "What part of New Jersey, are we in again?"

"New Brunswick, this is where the state's university is." I said.

"Nicole tells me you're quite the young playwright," Nathan said.

"I dabble," Cyril said.

Cyril's body language let me know, he was not comfortable with Nathan. He sensed something was up, something he wasn't going to like.

"Have you ever thought about writing for the movies?" Nathan asked.

"No," Cyril's answer was terse.

He next handed us each a glass of wine.

"Young man," Nathan said. "Let me put my cards on the table. Nicole here has been singing your praises. You've got a ground floor opportunity that any writer would kill for. Skyscraper

Studios, has projects in mind for several of your scripts and future plans for the rest. I am ready to represent you in this matter. And you will be set for the rest of your life."

"Sorry, my work..." Cyril gave me a hard look, "is for the stage and not the screen."

"Don't be foolish Cyril," Nathan said. "Theater's a dead medium."

"I guess that makes me an undertaker," Cyril said. Because I'm not allowing my work..."

"It will still be your work," Nathan said. "You can keep all the stage rights. Skyscraper only wants the movie rights."

"And when they get ahold of these so-called movie rights. They can do with them whatever they want?"

"A movie is not a play young man..."

"Sorry, I'm not interested."

"Cyril," I interjected. "There offering you fifteen million dollars. Most playwrights never get to earn a living at it. After that, you'd never worry about anything again. What an incredible validation of your work."

He looked at me with those penetrating Mediterranean eyes of his. "No sequels and they have to keep it exactly how I wrote it, no changes what so ever and that includes Standing Beside my Fire"

"That's impossible," Nathan said. "There's already an army of Script doctors set to re-work Standing by My Fire for the screen."

"My work doesn't need any doctors."

"You can't be that stupid," Nathan said.

I could sense Cyril's anger rising. Still calm he said. "I don't like being called stupid! You've been in my home long enough get out."

"What would you expect me to call someone who's about to let a fortune fly out his window?" Nathan was yelling. "You are an untested and unknown writer. I come all this way to bring you an offer and represent you."

"You didn't come all this way to represent me." Cyril said. "You came all this way to represent yourself. I may suffer from dyscalculia, but I know ten percent of fifteen million dollars is a million and a half dollars. Sorry, my work belongs to me. I suggest you go out the door before I make you go out the window."

"How New Jersey of you." Nathan sneered.

"I'm from Brooklyn."

As he exited, Nathan looked me in my face. I could tell he was angry and I would hear it later. "I'm taking the limo back to Manhattan. I'm sure you can find your way back. This is what happens when you involve yourself with someone not from the business."

"This someone," Cyril shouted at the leaving Nathan. "Will never be from that business!"

Worse than the annoyed look on Nathan's face was the anger I saw in Cyril's eyes.

"How dare you bring that charlatan here to try to financially strong arm me out of Standing Beside my Fire?"

"What," I shouted. "That wasn't my intention."

"Where to you get off, soliciting my stuff all over Hollywood without my permission. Do you know how many phone calls, texts and emails I've been getting from agents, directors and producers since this morning? How did they find my work and more importantly how did they find me!"

"Cyril your work is all over Amazon, e-bay and Barnes and Noble.com anyone can get a hold of it, I'm sure if they google you or one of your titles..."

"You don't care about Standing by My Fire," he said. "You just want to use it as a vehicle for your irrational self-interests at the expense of me and my work."

"That's not true!"

"I'm going for a walk. Don't be here when I get back." He said as he slammed the door.

FIVE

After a nasty shouting match with Nathan replete with recriminations. I realized Cyril was right. The contents of his work meant nothing to Nathan. All Nathan cared about was his million and a half dollar cut and what he was most furious about was he was not going to get it. Cyril, from Nathan's perspective had no right not to take the deal because he was depriving Nathan of his easy windfall. It was also inconceivable to Nathan as it would be to most movie people that someone would turn down fifteen million dollars to maintain the integrity of their work.

What pained me most about all of this; I finally realized just what that work had meant to Cyril. It was his medal of honor, his symbol of victory. It was proof to himself that he had power and authority over his dysgraphia and he'd conquered it.

At first, I thought it better to forget everything including Cyril. I couldn't, his face was in my thoughts and I yearned for his healthy laugh and the unencumbered freshness of his outlook on things. Mostly, I missed him and his conversation. I could listen to him for hours upon hours.

I tried repeatedly to call, text, and email him. All went unanswered. I began to worry a bit.

I called Jenine, she said she hadn't seen or spoken to him but he emailed her a cover he'd just designed for her. She also knew he was typesetting another professor's manuscript.

I'd be lying to myself, if I didn't admit that I was hoping there still might be some chance of doing Standing Beside my Fire. True, it would never be a film. Maybe it was time I got my ass back on a stage.

It was early Sunday morning, and Cyril still had not returned any of my calls. Jenine hadn't seen or heard from him since he emailed her the cover proof. She also told me if she lost her typesetter, she would never forgive me. I kept thinking about how I invaded his orderly life and disrupted it for irrational self-purposes.

After decades on Hollywood's 'A' list. I was used to getting my way. People with integrity was not something I encountered and even if I did, until meeting Cyril, I'd have considered a person's integrity a minor inconvenience that needed to be put aside so I could have my way.

With Cyril still my obsession, I decided to read the only thing of his I hadn't his eight-hundred-page fantasy novel. A fascinating yarn about a blind prince who must rely on his intellect alone to save his realm from an invading army of wizards, like everything else Cyril wrote, it captivated me.

I don't know what impulse came over me that made me rent that car, put on my wide brim winter hat, dark glasses and head to New Brunswick. Though I very much wanted to talk to Cyril, I was afraid to encounter him. I did the only thing I could do. Getting her number from Jenine. I called the only other person that I was familiar with who knew Cyril. Professor Carlisle, she'd agreed to meet with me in her home.

Though vibrant, she looked older up close, but not aged, just worn from the standard trials of life, she was in her late seventies and as sharp as a tack.

After the initial: "I'm so thrilled to meet you Ms. Davenport and I loved you in…" We began to speak.

"My dear," she said now at ease with me. "There are many people both in academia and in various other professions, who emphatically hold the opinion there is no such thing as creative genius.

They're wrong Cyril proves it."

"Are you saying Cyril is a genius?"

"I am. Not all geniuses are physicists and mathematicians. Have you read his fantasy novel?" "Yes" I said, and then she continued.

"Mister Tolkien, a university professor took decades to write his Lord of the Rings. Cyril, a learning-disabled high school dropout with almost no education, did his in a year. The math speaks for itself. Nobody in academia is ever going to admit Cyril is a genius, he's the wrong profile and because of his learning disabilities, they won't have to. I know with all certainty if I've met one genius in my life its Cyril Incromona."

"I don't understand what you're saying" I didn't.

"Nicole," she said, "May I call you Nicole?"

"Of course."

"Let me put it into perspective for you. There are geniuses all around us. We just don't notice them. For years, I had three stubborn stains on my tub, couldn't get them out, I had professionals come they couldn't remove them either.

While having a new sink installed a Polish man, who barely spoke English said: "No good, I clean." Ignoring him, I said sure take your best shot. When I came back upstairs, the stains were gone. I have no idea what he did because I didn't see it and when I asked him, he couldn't tell me because he didn't speak English. Geniuses find ways to solve things."

"I don't understand how that relates to Cyril," I said.

She sighed before she spoke. "There are two opposing interests in literature and the American book industry. Academia, which tries its best to maintain control over content. Then there are the big seven publishing houses, and by proxy literary agents who get books to market.

We academics object to the crap the big seven puts out. They in turn reject our work as unsalable and uncommercial. That forces us in academia to self-publish a terrible stigma and a costly venture; that is, till U-Publish-it comes along. But we're not there yet. With U-Publish-it, you're responsible for typesetting your work and your cover. And being academics, we'd never do all that. Never mind we're above such folly. U-Publish-it is not for us.

About a year ago just after my publisher dropped me. One of my students, Cyril's ex- fiancé brings me one of his novels. Turns out this obscure young man is typesetting his own work and designing his own covers. Even better, for a reasonable price, he'll share his knowledge.

Cyril liberated every one of us; we were no longer subjected to rejection by the publishing industry for being uncommercial. We could get our work to market without the expense of traditional self-publishing. Few of my colleagues want to admit that someone so much on the outside, who taught himself to do so many things, had that much power over us. None of us would have ever thought to learn how to typeset, no, not us where above that. That someone else's job. But Cyril did it for his work and told both the publishing industry and academia to shove it. And we, the literary leaders in this area, now had to rely on this high school dropout to make our work publishable.

As several of us got to know him. It became very uncomfortable when we learned Cyril, uneducated and burdened with dysgraphia could compose a book in considerably less time and more efficiently than any one of us. Worst of all, with Cyril typesetting for us, we could no longer blame big publishing for our shortcomings.

With him turning out his own well written novels while being burdened with learning disabilities. We had to stop hiding behind the comfort of our excuses. There are some professors here who Cyril typesets for, that despise him. They say it's because of his political and economic views. Bullshit, they don't like it that someone such as Cyril has such enormous power. But they'd dare not offend him, because he's the typesetting, cover designing goose with the golden egg.

Cyril Incromona for me was a game changer. More importantly than all of that. My books are mine again. No publisher can bully or pressure me anymore. Cyril gave me back my integrity as a writer and more. He rescued my work for me. From my perspective, that's a genius and a hero. So, what if he can't add up a column of numbers, or write out a check. I maternally love Cyril and when I saw his inability to write long hand, I suspected something was askew. It was at my urging he was finally tested and evaluated as a twice exceptional."

"So, you were the one who first noticed it, "I said.

"I'm sure I wasn't the first to notice it. Just the first to realize what he accomplished first."

I could tell she was reading my body language.

"You've wounded him, haven't you?" She said

"Yes, he won't return my calls."

"With all due respect, she said. "Cyril's twenty-four, aren't you a bit mature for him."

"In reality he may be a bit mature for me."

"I don't want you hurting him. I know all about what happened with him and my former student and her nasty father. I gave that man some phone call; whether he understood me or not I don't know. I used profanity as I'd never before. How dare he treat Cyril in such a manner!"

"Professor," I said. "You've been wonderful; do you know where Cyril is now?"

She looked at her watch, "Its 3:04, I would imagine he's ushering the Oedipus Rex matinee over at the Livingston Avenue Theatre."

"Thank you, I'll never find parking in downtown New Brunswick now. May I leave my car in your driveway?"

"Of course, she said but you'd better hurry, there doing this version as a one act and they should be nearly finished."

In spite of the wind blowing my hat off twice, and bitter winds ripping at my face, I managed to run the nearly two miles from Professor Carlisle's on the other side of the river in Highland Park, to the theater.

The play, I judged from the time should be letting out at any moment. I stood hoping Cyril wouldn't exit through one of the stage doors. If he didn't come out soon, I would use my celebrity to find out where he was. I was about to do that when Cyril exited the front entrance with another usher.

"See you tomorrow night," Calvin he said.

"Cyril," I bellowed.

"Oh, it's you," he said. "Nice hat, is Robert Sherwood holding auditions?"

"Very funny." I said.

"I want to talk to you."

"I'm still pissed at you," he said. "…bringing that carpetbagger to my home."

"He's not a carpetbagger, and though you might find him distasteful. He took a huge gamble on you then had to go back to Skyscraper with egg all over his face. I would think someone so obsessed with capitalism could see that."

"Nonsense, he wasn't doing it out of the goodness of his heart. He's a looting moocher who saw a way to abscond with someone else's work. And turn a quick buck. That has little to do with capitalism."

"Hey look! It's Nicole Davenport!" A passerby's voice shouted out.

"No, it's not," Cyril answered. "This is Gertrude Offenbacher from Old Bridge. She just looks like her. What the hell would Nicole Davenport be doing freezing here in New Brunswick yelling at me?" The bewildered passerby kept going.

"Nicole," he said. "Why are you here? I will never allow any of my plays to be made into films and that's final. I've already turned down fifteen million dollars. I don't know what else you could come up with?"

"Fuck you Cyril Incromona, I wish I could fucking hate you."

"What's stopping you," he shouted back, catching the attention of several pedestrians.

"You are, you fucking Genius."

71

"Complements," he chuckled. "That's and odd way to express one's contempt for another."

"It's not contempt you shit, its envy."

"Envy, envy—from what?"

"You owe your genius to nobody but yourself. My God, what total intellectual freedom you have. It's all yours pal nobody can lay claim on your brilliance. Everyone else I've ever known is the fucking product of what they've been taught. Not you, you bastard, you're the product of what you've learned on your own. That's so much better. Whenever I read your stuff or see you, I'm reminded the thoughts in my head may not be mine, but could have been placed there by professors and teachers with agendas. You instead, sought the facts then discerned the truth unencumbered by other people's noisy bullshit.

If only I could walk away from you. But I can't because you're the most noble being I've ever fucking encountered. You bastard how your words have changed me. You fucking mental Pimp. I've been intellectually gangbanged by your novels and plays. I've taken it up the mental ass from your poems. You've made me your literary bitch. What the hell did you do to me!"

He looked back at me with those Mediterranean eyes of his and said, "What I did to you was nothing. All that happened is you discovered art for art's sake. There's no consensus here my dear and that frightens the hell out of you. You're being forced to like my work on its own merits and even more painful, you've done that from your own judgment and that scares the crap out of you. There's no director here to guide you how to feel, there's no clip notes or reviews of my work to help you form an opinion. You admire my work from your soul. But you can't take possession of it for fear it will take possession of you."

"It's already taken possession of me you bastard!" I shouted back.

"No, it hasn't and it can't because it's mine. I won't give it permission to do that. It's ok to love something you don't own Nicole. The worst form of abuse there is, is trying to control something you love that isn't yours."

"Exactly!" I shouted at him. "And that's why you won't' allow a movie of Fire. Because you love it too much not to have control over it, you philosophical hypocrite, your terrified if you let it go it won't be yours anymore." He looked at me and for the first time I noticed a vulnerability in his face.

And then a level of hostility rose in him that I'd never seen.

"Are you fucking learning disabled too," he shouted back at me. "Fire was written to be performed on a stage not in front of a camera. There are no movie rights, they don't exist and as long as I live, they never will."

He started walking away.

"Cyril, wait," I shouted and he stopped dead. "Forget Fire. The real reason I'm here is because I missed you."

Cyril ran up to me, for a moment I wasn't sure what his reaction would be. "Thank God you said that, Nicole. I miss you too, I was too afraid to take your calls because I thought you were going to confront me about throwing that jerk out of my house."

"No," I said as I put my hand on his cold face. "All I wanted was to be with you."

"Let's get out of here," he said. "I've got some hot chocolate back at the apartment."

SIX

Unlike in his living room, there were blinds on the window in Cyril's bedroom. After a long hot chocolate and some tears and apologies from both of us. We found ourselves in his bed till we fell asleep. Now awake and standing by the blinds nude, tiny streams of light from the city outside reflected on Cyril's back and butt.

"You're awake," he said.

"Yes," I answered, as he got back into bed.

"Its cold up here," he said.

"It doesn't help when you're buck naked," I said.

"I prefer to think of it as exposed." He said. "And I'm about to expose something else to you."

"What."

"My Dream."

"I hope it wasn't a nightmare."

"Not that kind of dream. My dream is," he said with a crack in his voice. "Is to have Fire fully staged. I'd love for you to play the part."

"Cyril, you have my undivided attention."

"I'm not talking about a movie."

"I got you Cyril."

"The artistic director of the Livingston Avenue Theatre knows I'm a playwright. And like everyone else in the theater community in New Brunswick, he knows you and I have been seeing each other. He asked for a copy of Standing Beside my Fire. He says even though he despises the subject person of the play. He says the play has merit. If you'll commit to a three-week run, he'll put it up. He said the one hurdle is financing."

"I'll use my own money," I said. "But I select the director. And the house still has to pay you and you get a share of the receipts."

"That's doable," he said.

During the weeks of rehearsal, I thought it would be very Noël Coward like if I, the lead actress stayed with Cyril the playwright at his apartment. Even better than that, were the wonderful whispers backstage about he and I sleeping together.

Cyril went from excited with anticipation to near panic as opening night approached. Several times during the rehearsal, Cyril was needed to tweak his script for staging purposes. He would, and then he'd go to the upper seats stay for just a moment and rush out of the theater. Worried about him, I took a break and went back to his apartment. He was in bed with the pillow over his head sweating.

"Darling what is it," I said.

"I can't do this, I'll get you back all your money, only please don't make me go through this."

"Cyril, we open in four days. There's no turning back."

"No! I'm going to make a fool of myself. I'm no writer, I never was."

"Calm down," I said. "You're a wonderful writer."

"No, I'm not. I can barely spell my own name. I'm a fraud. This is all bullshit."

He turned his body away from me and I touched his bare shoulder. It was on fire from his nervousness.

"Suppose they hate it, and they trash it."

"I thought you said your work was yours and what people thought of it was immaterial?"

"I never should have exposed myself to all of this. Things were fine the way they were."

"No, they weren't Cyril," I said. "You can feign artistic detachment all you want in the end we're all still social beings. And we need that connection. The subject of your play after she wrote her magnum opus got a vicious review in a magazine that should have supported her novel. That critique drove her to her bedroom for days. Even the most noted practitioner of individual achievement got her feelings hurt. You're no different. And sweetheart, whether you like it or not all artist if they're men they have to metaphorically unzip their flies, the same way women artist have to open their blouses. And once you do that, you become worried that the world will know if your tits are too little or your dick is too small."

He turned to me and all I saw were his eyes. "I don't want to do this," he said.

"Why not," I said. "You're beautiful Cyril. You have this uncorrupted intellect that takes in everything around it, discerns it, and then enriches it into this simple and understandable truth. Fire may, as you say belong to you. But there's no crime in sharing it with the rest of us."

"No!" his voice was panicked. "I'm nothing but a freak of nature, without a computer I can't write out a check. I can't even count my change from the supermarket. Why did God do this to me! He couldn't just leave me with one or the other—no! He messed with me. If I'd known about being learning disabled earlier...I never would have written..."

"Are you blind too?" I shouted. "You don't see all that God has done for you. How old were you when you started writing?"

"Thirteen."

"How many plays and novels were written before you found out you were a twice exceptional?"

"Nine plays and four novels."

"Nine plays and four novels from the time your thirteen till your twenty-two. And you don't see the wonderful gift God gave you?"

"I don't."

"Men, you're all so dense," I said. "God shielded you. As you just said. If you had found out you had dysgraphia as a boy, you wouldn't have written a word. And the world now would not be anticipating something new and something fresh, written by a man who taught himself everything. I don't know anyone else who gets to wear that distinction."

"It's happened before," he said. "Miguel Pinero."

"Apples and oranges." I shouted. "Cyril everything you've put up with in your life was meant to bring you to this moment. Don't you understand you've climbed Mount Everest in your bare feet? Greatness my love, can be ignored, but it can't be denied and it won't stay put. All of this will be ok. More than that, it will be wonderful. I promise you."

I hated leaving him, but I had to get back and I made him promise he'd leave the apartment take his car and get himself out of New Brunswick. It was funny how suddenly my entire world had become that small city on the Raritan River. I was living there, working there, and my lover was there. I should have minded it and been homesick for Manhattan or LA, I wasn't not one bit. In reality, I was enjoying myself and had no problem strolling these streets again, as I did in my college years.

I'd be lying if I said I wasn't a bundle of nerves on opening night. I hadn't been on a stage in many years and I'd be on the stage of the Livingston Avenue Theater alone. Cyril and I had lunch together and he could barely speak, he was white as a ghost. I worried he wouldn't show up. Miguel Pinero, one of his favorite playwrights was arrested on the opening night of his play Short Eyes for snatching purses. William Inge, another favorite of Cyril's spent the opening night of Comeback Little Sheba in a bar somewhere in the vicinity of the Booth Theater.

The show must go on. I told myself and in spite of the fact that I had visions of him staggering through the streets of New Brunswick. I could no longer worry about Cyril, there was a play about to go up. With him out of my mind and heading to make my entrance. I was informed that the playwright was in attendance.

I don't know if the packed house was filled with devotees of the subject of the play, subscription holders or fans of mine. At its conclusion. They were on their feet cheering and whistling. The house lights came up. I couldn't see him, and then I looked at a spot in the sixth row where with Jenine on one side of him and professor Carlisle on the other, Cyril was clapping softly and I knew his claps were for me.

"Ladies and Gentleman!" I shouted. "Your Playwright Cyril Incromona." He took a meek bow.

Modesty, I thought, the person I just portrayed would be annoyed for such humility. The applause thundered again and he took a bigger bow.

"Thank you," he sounded timid. "Thank you," he said it again as he wiped his left eye and I realized then that I was madly in love with him.

EPILOGUE

The notices in New Jersey for Fire were excellent. Just before we took the play to Philadelphia, Cyril and I married. Next, we did Fire downtown, with series financial backing it moved to Broadway's Lorett Taylor Theater, where after nearly a year and a half and two other actresses assuming the role the play was still running.

Cyril's most recent offer for the film rights by someone representing one of my rival actresses was five million dollars. Cyril, again—refused. Two more of Cyril's plays have previewed out of town: one in Los Angeles, the other in Baltimore. His chess play: Kings' Knight 4 recently opened in San Francisco to raves. Several composers had approached him about turning that piece into a live musical for television featuring a particular teen idol. To their irritation, Cyril declined.

I wished I could have been there to support Cyril. My presence would have distracted the conference goers. Instead, I would support my husband through Skype.

As dynamic as Cyril was, things like addressing a formal crowd made him nervous. I could see his apprehension as he left this morning for the forty-five-minute drive from Central Park West to somewhere in Connecticut.

"Ladies and gentleman" my heart skipped a beat when the conference moderator began speaking. "We have a special guest. Like so many of us Twice Exceptionals, he wasn't evaluated till adulthood. This individual didn't let anything stand in the way of his dream, with dogged determination and his own vision; this young man who suffers with dysgraphia did the impossible. It is my privilege to introduce to you Pulitzer Prize and Tony award winning dramatist Cyril Incromona."

Cyril was nervous, but as he did at the Tony awards, he held it together. A chill ran up my spine as he began speaking.

"Friends," he said. "I'd like to thank you all for inviting me. I wrote out a bunch of notes in long hand, but I can't read my own handwriting. And even if I could, I don't have the ability to read aloud."

The crowd chuckled and I was glad that put Cyril at ease. He continued.

"Like so many of you here today, do in similar circumstances. I'll do this off the cuff. Nobody's better at faking it till making it than us, but when we make it, we make it faster, more efficiently and more profound, than anyone. We won't stop there. We'll develop a strategy to market it. We'll come up with the ideal branding campaign for it, the right demographic to sell it to; next, we'll show others how to operate it. We will then analyze its competition. And we'll refine it still more, to make it more competitive. We'll do all this before the age of twenty, while failing a math and spelling test. And that, is always followed by, you're not trying hard enough, you're so smart, you should be able to do this one two three. Why are you so lazy? The one thing we are not my friends—is lazy!"

I became choked up as the room let out a thunder of applause. And a grin came across Cyril's face.

"Thank you," he said. "As everyone in this room knows. I am a writer and I am also a twice exceptional with both dyscalculia and dys-graphia. Here's the interesting thing. I discovered I was a writer long before I discovered I was a twice exceptional. Upon the success of my play with my lovely wife Nicole, many people have wondered how someone with Dysgraphia could write anything, let alone a Tony award winning drama. There is a simple answer. I never let it get in my way. When they say that's impossible, I remind them Beethoven was deaf. Then I bring up Ray Charles, Stevie Wonder and Jose Feliciano.

There are no excuses, if you have vision and you have determination you will do it. Nobody knows better than I do when you have to fill out an employment application and your hand and arm become stiff. Not from fear but from a dys-function in your brain and rapidly your writing becomes unreadable to everyone including your-self. Then I think of the jobs I couldn't do. I could never be a waiter, bank teller, supermarket cashier or anything directly involving spelling and arithmetic.

That doesn't mean I can't write books. That doesn't mean I can't design a cover; it doesn't mean I can't become the VP of sales. It doesn't mean I can't be an educator. And watch out, be-cause like all of you in this room, when I do something, it's done better, brighter and more elegant than before.

True, it may take me a good hour to find my keys and wallet or get an accurate count of the money in that wallet. That's where it ends my friends, because nothing is in our way. We climb the highest ladders with lots of heavy baggage. And when we reach the top, the top is never the same, because on the way up, we've evaluated that latter in our heads and we've figured out how to make the top of that ladder safer, more comfortable and even more esthetic.

Remember your greatest asset is your biggest default, because it forced you to see everything from a perspective that was sharper and laced with an infinite-colored spectrum only you could see. And when you apply that exclusive knowledge, you're unbeatable. And above it all, what we twice exceptionals have accomplished we did on our own and it belongs to each one of us. Thanks for letting me be the key note speaker at this conference on twice exceptionals."

The crowd was applauding again and Cyril looked right at me and said. "I think I did it."

"Yes, you did my darling."